A Land of Promise Adventure | Book 2

The MISADVENTURE of the BLUSTERY WIND

A Land of Promise Adventure | Book 2

The MISADVENTURE of the BLUSTERY WIND

by: Shellie Wooten
Illustrated by: Channing Davis

Published by IngramSpark
https://www.ingramspark.com
One Ingram Blvd.
La Vergne, TN 37086

Library of Congress Cataloging-in-Publication Data
Scripture quoted by permission. All Scripture quotations are from the NET Bible® copyright ©1996, 2019 by Biblical Studies Press, L.L.C. http://netbible.com All rights reserved.

ISBN PAPERBACK: 978-1-7368437-4-1

Cover Design and Illustrations by Channing Davis
Edited by Robert Mims
Editorial Design by Kelsey Langenegger

More information about the Land of Promise books visit:
www.landofpromisebooks.com

Printed in the USA

To Pop - thank you for being an inspiration for the character. You are always willing to teach, instruct, and pour into the next generation. You lead in love and wisdom.

To my cherished friendships - reminding me that we are better when we work together. We've accomplished many amazing moments in our lives and I can't imagine life without the blessing of having you in it! Christie, Angie, Kari, Betty, Pat, Becky, Megan, Kiki, and Natasha, thank you for being my rock in moments I needed a friend. You believed, encouraged, and cheered me on and I am so grateful for you!

To my Lord Jesus Christ - He is the reason I love!

TABLE OF CONTENTS

Land of Promise Friends   11

Prologue | Fear Finds a Voice   15

Chapter 1 | Safety First   18

Chapter 2 | Friend…Foe…or Fear   23

Chapter 3 | Anticipation   28

Chapter 4 | Mischievousness Gone Wrong   33

Chapter 5 | Heat Always Rises   38

Chapter 6 | Mapping a Landing   44

Chapter 7 | Make a Memory   48

Chapter 8 | Dusty Roads   54

Chapter 9 | Losing Altitude   58

Chapter 10 | A Friend Called Mischievous   61

Chapter 11 | Down to the Treetops   64

Chapter 12 | Adventurers Descend   69

Epilogue | Sing it Again   74

Parent & Teacher Helps   79

LAND OF PROMISE FRIENDS

Welcome to the Land of Promise, where everyday adventures turn into meaningful lessons. Through friendship, courage, creativity, and faith, a group of kids learn how to work together, face challenges, and trust God—even when things don't go as planned.

The Land of Promise series is filled with heart, humor, and hope—bringing the Fruit of the Spirit to life through engaging stories kids love and lessons families value.

But the fruit of the Spirit is love, joy, peace, patience, kindness, goodness, faithfulness, gentleness, and self-control.

Galatians 5:22-23
The Bible, New English Translation

Charity is super sweet and a little shy. Once you get to know her, you will find out how much she loves life and her friends. She isn't the best at cooking but she will definitely be there to help you clean up.

JoJo knows how to get the party started. She is fun to be with and enjoys celebrating with her friends. She may forget to do a few chores now and then, but she will never forget your birthday party!

Quill is always chill. He knows how to keep his world peaceful. He will always reassure you when a situation becomes difficult. He may not pick sides in a fight but he will choose peace for the win!

Patience is a great friend to have. She will wait for you after school or when you are the last one off of the bus. She always knows when you need a hug. She's very artistic and will paint you a picture on a rainy day.

Kindly lives on a farm and loves to grow vegetables. He is very generous with everything he owns. If you can't find him, check the garden and if he's there, he'll have some veggies ready for you to take home to your family.

Goody is ready for anything. He doesn't go anywhere without his backpack of essentials. He loves skateboarding and fixing things. Whenever trouble comes, Goody usually has a tool to fix it. If it's good advice you need, he has that too.

Faith is a planner. She loves to be organized and ready for anything. She is athletic and loves to run and play sports. Although she likes to win, if you play a game with her, she will encourage you to do your best.

Gen is creative and able to befriend the most difficult of people. She loves flowers and surrounding herself with beauty. Don't be surprised if she makes you a paper flower and hides it in your desk. She may be quiet, but she is always listening.

Temperance is super smart and will find the positives in every situation. He is calculated when making a decision and will offer you the best path to take. You can trust Temperance because he is trustworthy.

PROLOGUE

FEAR FINDS A VOICE

Do not be overcome by evil, but overcome evil with good.
Romans 12:21

Being afraid can make you do crazy things. You might run away from a fuzzy spider, yell into the darkness when you can't see, or stand paralyzed on the diving board at the pool when the water seems miles away.

For Feargus, fear pushed him to be naughty. He found he was afraid in most situations, from making friends to walking into a playground full of kids. He didn't start out being naughty and he didn't start out being afraid, but when life didn't go his way he decided one way to take control was to to cause problems for those around him. If Feargus could control a problem by being naughty, then that was the choice he would make.

As time went by, Feargus learned he liked the attention he received when he did pranks. Even though it made people upset and frustrated, he didn't mind. He wanted to appear to be tough, strong, and confident, but since he struggled to find his place, he liked making others feel uncomfortable.

Because of his choices, Feargus didn't make friends, not one. One thing that Feargus did make was trouble. He seemed to

be scheming all of the time, looking for ways to be a bother
to everyone. His favorite target was anyone who had a friend
because that was something he didn't have.

When the bell rang, it wasn't unheard of for Feargus to drop
his pencil case full of pencils making the kids around him trip
and fall on the scattered pencils that littered the floor. Feargus
would laugh, but he was the only one who thought it was funny.

There were some brave kids who had tried to be friends with
him. Some of the ones who tried the hardest became Feargus's
biggest targets. Feargus would spray water on them at the
drinking fountain or wad up their homework and throw it
out the school window. Eventually, no one tried anymore. He
became known as the boy to stay away from.

CHAPTER 1

SAFETY FIRST

*Do not be anxious about anything. Instead, in every situation,
through prayer and petition with thanksgiving,
tell your requests to God.*
Philippians 4:6–7

The sun was beginning to display brilliant hues of pink and
orange across the sky when the Land of Promise friends arrived
at Wildflower Field. Quill, Charity, Goody, Temperance, JoJo,
Patience, Faith, Kindly, and Gen were bustling with excitement.

Several days before, they had decided to embark on a new
adventure together, riding across the Land of Promise in
Goody's family's hot air balloon.

You see, today was launch day for the Land of Promise Festival
of Balloons. The ground was littered with vibrant, colorful hot
air balloon nylon being unrolled and spread out all over the
lush green grass of Wildflower Field. Anyone who had a hot air
balloon showed up to enjoy the day and festivities.

Goody's Grandpa, who Goody and nearly everyone in the Land
of Promise called "Pop," was happy to take Goody's friends
up in their hot air balloon. Going up in the hot air balloon
had become a tradition for Goody's family each year at the
Festival of Balloons. Goody was excited to share this amazing

experience with his best buds.

The friends had agreed to arrive a little early to go over all the safety instructions before the launch. Goody arrived a couple of hours before his friends; just before the sun had begun to warm the ground. He wanted to help Pop with unloading the deflated balloon off the back of his pop's trailer. Goody started feeling a little tired from the morning preparations but when his friends arrived, he was refueled with energy, excited to show the balloon to everyone.

Pop had begun inflating the hot air balloon when he turned to see Goody chatting excitedly with his eight friends. They were staring wide-eyed at this huge balloon laying out on the lawn, basket on its side.

JoJo spoke first, "Holy cow, Goody! It's so much bigger than I ever thought possible! This is so super duper cool! I can't believe we are going up, up and away in a piece of fabric filled with gas and fire!"

Kindly, who likes his bare feet planted firmly on the ground, began stammering, "JoJo, don't say it like that! I am already nervous to be floating through the air in a hot air balloon. Goody, do we get to wear parachutes?"

Goody teased, "No, my friend, I hope you brought some wings."

Kindly chuckled nervously then looked around the group of friends and asked again, "So, do we get our own parachutes? I am not sure I feel confident with just fabric holding all of us up without a backup plan."

Pop, who was still working on inflating the balloon, chuckled overhearing Goody tease Kindly.

Pop was a tall man with gray and white hair and a silver and black mustache and beard that seemed to shimmer in the early morning sun. Although his posture was bent from years of hard work, he was much taller than the group of friends, standing head and shoulders above everyone.

Walking over to the group, Pop's deep and steady voice began calming down the nervousness in everyone. "You are all very brave young men and women and today's events will possibly change your life forever! Experiencing a hot air balloon ride not only alters how you see the world, we realize how small we are and how big God is!" With this statement, Pop opened his large arms and hands to show how massive God is.

"We will take a few minutes to go over all of our balloon safety and a few how-to's. By the end of today, I want you to walk away with the knowledge of how a hot air balloon flies and how to navigate it. Never let a moment go by when you aren't learning something. Now let's circle up and say a prayer and then we will get started."

As the friends gathered around Pop, they instinctively joined hands. Goody and Kindly were on either side of Pop and everyone else joined hands one by one, completing their chain of friendship. Temperance placed his notepad on the ground in front of him.

Pop began praying over their day's travels, "Thank you God for your hand of protection over this group. Let us stay safe, enjoy the journey, trust in You, and lean on each other's strengths! Amen."

Once the prayer was over, Pop gave lots of details about how the balloon flies, what part each of them would play and how to stay safe throughout the day. Everyone listened intently. Temperance, who was enjoying every moment of learning, picked up his notebook and began taking detailed notes.

"The design of the balloon is pretty simple," Pop began, "you have the envelope, which is the nylon portion of the balloon, the vent that provides the heat, and the basket. Heat makes the balloon rise so we light the burners to fill the envelope. We anchor the basket to the ground with sand bags and stakes until we are ready to go."

As Pop was explaining all the details of how the hot air balloon works, as if the timing was perfectly planned, the basket rolled onto its base and the balloon was so full it looked as if were about to burst with color. The friends all turned their attention to the balloon and gasped. Standing so close to this hot air balloon, feeling the heat from the burner, and getting to be part of this adventure together was beyond anything they had ever experienced.

Pop continued with a few final instructions on how to stay safe and then they were all given tasks to get their launch site cleaned up before take-off.

CHAPTER 2

FRIEND...FOE...OR FEAR

*But I say to you who are listening: Love your enemies, do good to
those who hate you, bless those who curse you,
pray for those who mistreat you.*
Luke 6:27–28

From his vantage point, he could tell that everyone was already
having a great time and they weren't even up in the air yet. He
watched Pop instructing the group of friends and how they
seemed to hang on every word. Something about all of this
bothered him. Maybe it was the fact that they were all "buddy-
buddy." It could be that they were getting to ride in a hot air
balloon together. But mostly, he figured it was because they all
had each other. Feargus didn't have anyone.

The longer he watched, the more irritated he became. When
they joined hands to pray, a strange feeling inside Feargus
twisted into a devious plan. He was going to come up with a
way to ruin their day. He just had to come up with the perfect
moment to make his mischievous move.

Feargus had long since stopped asking himself why he wanted to
make trouble for everyone, and why he wanted to ruin all the
possible friendships around him. He speculated when he first
had those feelings. It was the summer before starting preschool
that Feargus' mom took him to their neighborhood park where

several kids were already playing.

Feargus never had a problem making friends but on this particular day, a couple of kids starting being quite mean towards Feargus when he asked, "Hey guys, wanna play on the jungle gym with me?"

One boy laughed and remarked, "Why would we want to play with you? You look weird and have ugly hair!"

Feargus didn't know how to respond. He had always made friends at the park. He couldn't figure out how he looked and what his hair had to do with playing.

He laughed nervously and said, "I just wanted to play. You don't have to be mean."

The second boy said, "Yeah, we will play with you, only if you shave your head and wear a paper bag over your head!"

The two boys laughed and ran off together, leaving Feargus standing alone wiping tears out of his eyes. A very sad Feargus ran over to his mom and demanded, "Mom, take me home! I don't want to play at the park!"

Puzzled, Feargus' mom took him home. When he ran into his room, he shut the door and threw himself over the bed and began sobbing in his pillow. When he stopped crying, he went over to his dresser mirror and stared at himself for the longest time.

Out of the silence, Feargus began talking to himself in the

mirror. "Feargus, that's it! You don't need to make friends. Forget everyone else."

When school started, Feargus never tried to befriend anyone. He was afraid that if he did try, he would be rejected. He didn't make any friends. He even began making it hard for those around him who tried to be nice to him.

Feargus's new goal was to make everyone as miserable as himself. Along with being mischievous, the newest targets all started when he was at the Promise Parade a few weeks back. One of the workers at the parade, Quill, had asked to borrow his scooter and then almost immediately after he asked, he didn't need it.

Unbeknownst to anyone around him, Feargus had decided that morning that he was tired of being alone and was going to try something new, to be kind. When he was approached by Quill, the parade worker, he knew that this was his moment. Not only would he save the day by loaning out his scooter, he had a chance to become friends with this young man.

Just as soon as his heroic moment was there, it was immediately snatched away when one of the girls in the parade, Charity, gave Quill her scooter. It made Feargus so angry. How thoughtless of her to steal this opportunity of friendship and fame.

He decided to find out all about these kids. It lead him to realize that there were nine kids who quickly became close friends the day of the parade. This made them the biggest and most rewarding target he had ever had. An opportunity to ruin so many friendships at the same time brought such satisfaction to his miserable goal.

He didn't fear being alone when he was busy being a nuisance.

He planned to keep an eye on these friends and when the moment was right, he would make his move.

CHAPTER 3

ANTICIPATION

Rely on the Lord! Be strong and confident! Rely on the Lord!
Psalm 27:14

As the sun continued to rise off of the horizon, it echoed that time was nearing for everyone to start their journey up and into the sky. Each hot air balloon had a timeframe they could take off within and keep a safe distance from each other. Pop's balloon was filled, and the fabric that once covered the grassy plain was completely off of the ground, bulging out from every seam into the strips of nylon, appearing to be soft pillows. The basket had begun to lift and tug on the ropes that held it down on the ground.

The balloon was so colorful. The top of the balloon looked like a bright yellow sun, and the sun rays shown down through various shades of blue. The bottom around the opening where the flame was lit, had flowers that cut into the blue hues. It was bright, beautiful, and gleamed happiness.

Sandbags and stakes at the base of the basket held the balloon as it hovered just off of the ground. One by one, each of the friends climbed a rope into the basket. First the girls, Charity, JoJo, Faith, Patience and Gen climbed up the rope ladder, one at a time, helping each other into the basket. Then the boys took

28

their turn. First came Temperance, then Quill, and lastly Kindly, each of them jumping in, causing the basket to shift with their weight and force. Everyone except Pop and Goody was on board.

Pop and Goody were finishing up with gathering a few items when Goody asked, "Pop, do you want me to run the tools back to the truck?"

Pop smiled at the group of friends all hanging out nervously in the basket and said to Goody, "Yeah, that sounds like a good idea, I'll join you." Then to the group he assures them with a warm smile, "We have a couple more things to do, and then, we will be off!"

Goody flung his backpack over his back and walked over to Pop who was bending over the lines that were tied down. Pop had begun the process to unhook the ropes that were securing the balloon when he said, "I need to grab the walkie-talkies out of my truck." He retied a rope he'd been working on and slowly got up and started walking back towards where the vehicles were parked.

Pop looked over at the friends in the basket and said, "You guys stay put and we will be right back. You won't go anywhere, all the ropes are still secure." Pop and Goody picked up a few odd items that were scattered about and headed back to the truck to tidy up their tools.

Kindly breathed a sigh of relief since they weren't leaving quite yet. Temperance was checking over the details of his notes. Quill was leaning with his back against the basket, looking over the field of balloons, already enjoying the amazing view. He didn't seem to be bothered by the fact that they were about to leave the ground and fly through the sky.

Charity and Gen were hugging each other and Charity exclaimed, "I can't believe we are actually going up in a hot air balloon! This is so exciting and scary all at the same time."

But Kindly, who had not stopped shaking, replied, "I can't believe I agreed to this. I like the ground and find it quite comforting to have my feet firmly planted on it or even in it!!"

Faith giggled, "It will be okay, Kindly, we will only be up for an hour or so and then you will be back in the dirt where your feet feel at home"

"That will be a relief," Kindly sighed.

Gen agreed, "Yes, Kindly, we will be fine. Besides, with Goody and Pop, I wouldn't worry a bit. They have done this so many times. They are pros! And look, Temperance took great notes, so we are in good hands."

Joy, who couldn't seem to hold her excitement to herself, blurted out, "I'm so nervous-cited!!"

Charity studied her for a moment, smiled, and said, "I don't think that is a word, JoJo."

"Sure it is, it's a word I use when I am a little nervous and I am little excited. I am nervous-cited!" Joy grabbed the edge of the basket and looked out toward where Goody and Pop had disappeared. "Do you think we are going to leave soon? I can't wait any longer!"

Quill said, "I am sure they had a little more to do to get us up in the air than they first thought. Everytime I work on a project, it seems to take longer than I first anticipated. I've learned to go with the flow."

Patience, who had been silently taking everything in, finally spoke up, "Oh JoJo, just think, the longer we wait, the more nervous-cited you will be for an even longer period of time." She continued, "I hope they are doing okay, it does seem like it is taking them a long time."

"In my estimation," Temperance stated as he was going over his notebook, "we should be up in the air in 10 minutes or less. With the winds at 10 miles per hour and the open field they are planning to land in, we should be back on the ground in one hour and 17 minutes."

"Wow, Temperance!" Gen exclaimed shaking her head in amazement, "That is so specific. You are so smart!"

"I don't like to guess when things happen, I like to know ahead of time what to expect and numbers usually tell us what we need to know, if we pay attention and do the math."

A few minutes had gone by and Pop and Goody had still not returned. The group of friends waited with excitement as they kept looking the direction Pop and Goody had disappeared. There was a mix of emotions in the basket, but everyone, except Kindly, couldn't wait to be in the air.

CHAPTER 4

MISCHIEVOUSNESS GONE WRONG

The one who conducts himself in integrity will live securely, but the one who behaves perversely will be found out.
Proverbs 10:9

Feargus had one goal in mind — to ruin the day for anyone having a good time. As Pop and Goody made their way toward the parked vehicles, Feargus turned his attention to the hot air balloon holding the eight friends awaiting the return of their guides.

He crouched low to avoid drawing any attention to himself and slinked over to where the sand bags weighted the balloon down. He stopped and sat against the basket of the balloon, relieved that he wasn't spotted. He took a moment to gather his thoughts as to what he could do to make the day miserable for these friends.

As he sat beside the basket, he overheard the group talking. He didn't recognize who was speaking, but he heard one of the boys say, "I hope they hurry up. I don't like being in the basket without Pop and Goody. They are the ones who really know how to make this thing go up. I know we did the training with Pop, but I can't remember anything he said!"

Feargus could hear how anxious the boy was, but all the others began encouraging him.

"Don't worry, Kindly, this will be a great day! You will see! Once we land, you will want to get right back up in the air again!"

"I am not sure about that, JoJo, this is a little more air-adventure than I am use to. I like ground-adventures that include dirt and getting dirty."

As they continued to discuss air versus ground adventures, Feargus had an idea. He could poke holes in the sand bags so that when they go to drop the sand bags to take off, they will be empty and hopefully cause some confusion on ascent. Pop will think that Goody did something wrong, and it may stir up some frustration.

Feargus grabbed one of the stakes and tugged on it to pull it out of the ground, then used it to poke some holes in a few of the sandbags around the base of the basket. He crouched down and crawled around out of sight as he poked the sandbags. The sandbags slowly emptied out leaving piles of sand beside the once full burlap sacks.

As he finished his moment of mischievousness, he rushed back over to his hiding spot to wait out the drama that he was sure would be entertaining.

Just then, a surprise, blustery wind came out of nowhere. The stake that Feargus had used to poke the sandbags still lay on the ground, un-staked. The sand bags that were full a few minutes ago, flopped and banged the side of the basket in the wind.

The balloon that had been weighted down before began to hover even higher, pulling at the remaining stakes that were still holding it down.

From inside the basket, Feargus heard a few squeals as the basket rocked back and forth in the wind. He could see the hands of the group hanging and grasping for leverage. Behind him, he heard the heavy feet of Pop and Goody running quickly towards the hot air balloon. They yelled at the group to turn down the flame, but no one heard over the squeals. Goody took the lead and increased his speed to attempt to get to the basket in time.

Quick thinking Goody launched a walkie-talkie through the air that landed squarely in the center of the basket, just missing Charity's head as it wizzed by. He continued to run towards the basket to try and grab the stakes that were beginning to pull out of the moist morning ground.

As Goody reached the first stake, he realized it was already loose and he attempted to stake it back down. Then the wind whipped up again and all the stakes were pulled from the ground, The stake Goody was holding was yanked out of his grip and the balloon had officially launched. The balloon quickly ascended and bobbed in the wind. It was raising too fast for anyone to stop it.

Pop had finally caught up to Goody and grasped onto Goody's shoulder to hold himself up as he tried to catch his breath. They both stared up at the balloon that was beginning to grow smaller as the wind carried them away. Feargus heard Pop yell up to the balloon with assurance, "Grab your walkie-talkie and remember your training! We will get you down."

Feargus, still hiding, began to sweat as he felt the seriousness of this decision to ruin the day for these kids. This isn't what he wanted or anticipated. He decided to quickly leave Wildflower Field so that noone would know he was the culprit. He wanted to go somewhere he could wait to find out how the hot air balloon and the gang inside would find their way down, one way or another.

CHAPTER 5

HEAT ALWAYS RISES

When I am afraid, I trust in you.
Psalm 56:3

In one moment, the kids were chattering about the flight and calming down Kindly. In the next, they were being tossed about by what felt like someone yanking and shaking up the basket. The group squealed, a walkie-talkie landed squarely in the center of the basket, and then they heard some unintelligible yelling outside the basket. The feeling of a tug, a swaying back and forth, and then, nothing. Just a calm gentle rise up into the air, suspended above the ground and below the clouds.

Even though the ascent at any other time would have been enjoyable, chaos and confusion took place in the basket of the hot air balloon as these eight young kids launched into their first unexpected solo flight.

All of the training was lost in the moment of pandemonium. Everyone except Kindly was clinging to the edge looking over the basket as the ground they were secured to a moment ago, shrunk to a miniature land as the balloon quickly rose. Kindly, who loved the dirt, was crouched down inside the basket, eyes squeezed closed and his hands grasping the floor of the woven fibers of the basket. Over and over again Kindly kept saying, "This can't be happening! This can't be happening!"

Temperance and Charity were on the side of the basket closest to the parking lot and they could see Goody and Pop down below running towards the launch site shouting up something that sounded like "walk" and "remember."

Temperance yelled back, "I didn't catch that. What did you say?" He turned his attention to Charity who also saw them and asked, "Did you understand Goody?"

Charity replied, "I'm not sure what he said, Temperance. I couldn't understand him."

When it was clear to the group they were up in the air and without any trained supervision, Temperance quickly took lead. He pulled out his notepad, which had meticulous notes from Pop's safety presentation. He turned to the first words he had written down.

Step 1 - Enjoy the journey.

Well, that wasn't happening at this particular time so he thought he better come back to that one later.

Step 2 - The burner controls the height of the balloon.

Temperance realized that without the sandbags and the weight of Pop and Goody in the basket, they needed to slow the ascent down some so that they didn't end up at the moon. Temperance was shorter and couldn't reach the lever to control the flame. Kindly was a little taller than the rest of the group and Temperance needed Kindly's height and farmhand strength to turn the burner down.

Temperance turned to Kindly, who was still grasping at the basket floor, "Kindly, I know this isn't exactly how you thought today would go, but when you are faced with something that is unpredictable on the farm, how do you work through it?"

Kindly replied, "When I'm on the farm, I'm on the ground, so I can think clearly in an unpredictable problem, while on the ground!"

Temperance chuckled, "Let's pretend we are on the ground and why don't you give me a hand with the flame. We need to turn it down a little so we don't float in the sky forever, so we can get to the ground again. Think you can help me out by reaching up and turning it down?"

Joy encouraged, "You can do this, Kindly. We all need you!"

Quill spoke up, "Yes, Kindly! You are the tallest and strongest so we need you to stand up and face your fear! You won't be disappointed. The view is amazing even with our current circumstance."

Charity reached down and grabbed Kindly's hand that was still flat against the base of the basket and pulled his hand up towards a standing position. As she did this she grabbed the walkie-talkie that was laying on the floor.

At that moment she realized what Goody was trying to tell them. Charity turned to Temperance and said, "Goody must have been saying walkie-talkie. He wants us to turn on the walkie-talkie." She handed the walkie-talkie to Faith who was standing next to her.

While Charity continued to coax Kindly to stand, Faith switched on the walkie-talkie. Almost at once the sound of a crackled voice was saying, "Come in, guys, can you hear me? Hello? Come in!"

Faith excitedly yelled out, "It's Goody!"

Temperance responded, "Answer him, Faith! Tell him we are all okay!"

Hearing Goody's voice gave Kindly the confidence he needed to fully stand as he continued to grip Charity's hand.

Faith squeezed the button to talk and replied, "Oh Goody, it is so good to hear your voice! We are all doing okay. A little shaken but we are good! What happened? Did we do something wrong?"

Goody's voice crackled a response, "We are still trying to figure out what happened but the main goal is to make sure you guys get down safe and sound. Over."

Everyone nodded in agreement. They all liked that idea.

Goody continued, "We need you to slow down your ascent. You need to lower the flame. Over."

Temperance nodded at Faith that he wanted to speak with Goody, and he grabbed the walkie-talkie from her. He spoke into the walkie-talkie, "Hey Goody, this is Temperance. We are currently working to bring down the flame. Kindly is the tallest, and he is building up the courage he needs to reach up to the burner. Over."

Goody responded, "That's great, Temperance! Kindly, you can do it! It's just like being on the ground but with a better view! You've got this! Once we get your ascent under control, we will work on your descent. Over."

Kindly, while still holding Charity's hand, eyes squinted closed, reached up with his other hand until he felt where the lever was and began slowly turning back the gas that gave the flame it's strength.

Charity smiled, "That's amazing, Kindly! You've got this!"

Temperance watched carefully and cautioned Kindly to turn the flame lever so that they lower slowly. When Temperance felt that the balloon had stopped rising, Kindly ceased turning the lever.

Temperance spoke over the walkie-talkie to Goody again, "Goody, we have the balloon at a place were it is no longer rising. What do we do next?"

Over the walkie-talkie, the group of friends could hear crackling and some garbled talking but nothing else.

Gen, who had been taking in this whole event silently, finally spoke up and calmly said, "The walkie-talkie must be out of range." She paused as she contemplated her next comment, "I think we may be on our own for the next part of the trip." She looked over at Temperance and breathed heavily. "Temperance, what did you write down as the next step in our journey?"

CHAPTER 6

MAPPING A LANDING

*Remember your leaders, who spoke God's message to you;
reflect on the outcome of their lives and imitate their faith.*
Hebrews 13:7

Known for always being prepared, Pop and Goody were surprised at the unexpected quick departure of the hot air balloon. They had taken precautions so something like this wouldn't happen. They would have never left the group alone in the basket if they suspected the balloon would launch prematurely.

Determining the cause was not a priority at this point. The most important item of business to Goody was making sure that the training that had taken place with his friends earlier in the day would provide them with the skills they needed, even through the chaos of doing it without Pop and him.

Goody was relieved once the group finally thought to turn on the walkie-talkie. He knew that they would only have a few moments before they were out of range so he was hoping someone would calm down enough to think to turn it on. Thankfully, Faith's calm voice answered his call.

While Goody gave some much needed guidance over the walkie-talkie, Pop was at work checking the wind direction and speed back at the truck. He pulled out his trusty well-worn map out of the truck's glove box to get the lay of the land, looking for open land where he projected they would be able to touch down. He had to work quickly. Pop and Goody needed to jump into the truck and try to follow as best as they could so that communication through the walkie-talkies could continue. They had to stay within a two mile radius to stay connected. With the balloon on the move, they were going to be out of range soon.

Pop motioned for Goody to make his way back to the truck so they could follow the misguided hot air balloon, to stay within range. Goody quickly jogged back to the truck, all the while, keeping his eyes toward where the hot air balloon quickly ascended higher and further away.

Goody was encouraging Kindly over the walkie-talkie and began giving some instructions about their descent when he realized they had stopped responding. Goody looked up at Pop with intensity and said, "Pop, we have to get within range. I don't want them to feel like they are up in the air all alone."

Pop said, "Well, they may be alone but with the training they had and our prayer over them, they will be fine. I know God has them in his hands."

Pop turned the engine key and the truck roared to life. He put the truck in gear and sped off toward the hot air balloon.

Pop said to Goody, "Here, take this old map I have of the Land of Promise and let's figure out where we can set those kids down."

"Okay, Pop!" Goody grabbed the map while Pop was driving towards the direction of the balloon, he and Goody began to discuss the next steps.

"Goody, once we get into range, radio up to them and have them check their altitude. Make sure they get it to a thousand feet and hold steady there as we work through where they will bring the balloon down. I need you to check the weather report to see how fast the wind is blowing."

Goody was holding the map and scanning the sky for his friends when he said to Pop, "We have to remember that we aren't in the basket as well so that is going to account for less weight. What we told them in the training will be off a little due to the math being wrong."

CHAPTER 7

STEP 3 - MAKE A MEMORY

I will remember the works of the Lord.
Psalm 77:11

Only a few minutes had passed but to the group it seemed like eternity. How long had it been since they were on the ground? Just a few minutes, but a few minutes ago they couldn't wait to be in the air. Now all they could think about was how to get safely back onto the ground.

Temperance was reading over the steps with everyone as Gen, Charity, Patience, Joy, and Quill were peering down over the sides of the basket to the ground below, amazed by the beauty they could see.

From the view of their basket they observed The Land of Promise. Hills grew smaller, houses looked like toys to play with, and the trees appeared to be a blanket of dark green broccoli instead of forests.

Quill exclaimed, "Everything looks so peaceful on the ground, but it has majorly shrunk in size."

Charity continued with her stunned observation, " Oh wow! Look around at the sky, guys. Can you see all the colorful hot air balloons beginning to rise?"

48

Kindly was sitting against the side of the basket with his knees pulled in tight, his arms hugging his legs. He had buried his head into his knees once his moment of bravery had concluded.

Joy crouched next to Kindly as she placed her hand on Kindly's shoulder to console him and said, "I know we have to figure out how we are going to get down but it is hard not to be so happy to see so many wonderful things from this view. I didn't realize how beautiful Land of Promise would be from up here. It is breath taking!" Still holding her hand on Kindly's shoulder, she stood up and took in the view.

Temperance had been reading aloud, but more for himself than for anyone to hear. He was saying, "And when we are up in the air, you must look around and make a memory."

"What did you say, Temperance?" asked Patience who had been listening quietly to all that Temperance was reading.

"It says that we should make a memory," Temperance responded.

"How can we make a memory that is good and lovely in the middle of feeling afraid?" asked Charity.

Joy answered, "When I am afraid, I like to sing a song to calm me down. What if we make up a song about flying in the hot air balloon?"

The group all smiled and nodded in agreement, everyone except Kindly, who of course was still sitting frightened on the floor of the basket.

Quill said, "Oh, JoJo, I think that is a great idea. Why don't you get us started with the first line of our flying song."

Joy started on a low note and ended on a high note when she began singing a charming tune, "When we fly in the sky where the clouds and birds go by…" She smiled and breathed in the fresh air as she looked for someone to take up the next phrase of the song.

Gen continued with the tune and sang a new line, "The wind controls the places we go…" She paused to see if someone could add to her line.

Quill laughed out a line as he sang, "Adventure awaits so enjoy the show!"

Everyone giggled, and they sang their song together as Temperance wrote down these new lyrics.

When we fly in the sky
Where the clouds and the birds go by
The wind controls the places we go
Adventure awaits so enjoy the show

Faith looked over to where Kindly was still hunkered against the basket, eyes buried behind his knees. Everyone was handling their predicament well, and she was beginning to feel bad that he wasn't part of the fun. She bent down and gave Kindly a hug and said, "Kindly, we are going to be alright, I know we are! You don't need to worry. Pop and Goody have already given us so much knowledge, and they will help us land safely."

Joy continued the encouragement, "I promise, if you open your eyes, you will see something amazing."

Something switched in the way Kindly was sitting. He raised up his head and shoulders and looked up to all his friends who stood around him, knees still shaking. At that moment, his face changed from fear to determination. Kindly stood up and for the first time really looked around the Land of Promise from this birds-eye view. He hugged Faith and said, "Thank you for not giving up on me. I will do my best to not allow my fear to keep me from helping us get to the ground safely."

Patience smiled knowingly. She believed that Kindly had the courage to overcome his fear and it showed up at just the right time. She began singing again the song they were making up, "When you fly in the sky we can't believe what we see with our eyes…."

Charity finished the verse with her line, "Our homes below, so tiny and small, mountains are hills, nothing is tall."

So again the group sang their second verse together:

When we fly in the sky
We can't believe what we see with our eyes
Our homes below, so tiny and small
Mountains are hills, nothing is tall

The group laughed out loud and cheered for making up a second verse. They sang their song together, both verses. Temperance sang out with confidence from the lyrics he had written down. Everyone felt a bit of relief and was grateful for

making this memory together as they floated through the open skies, nothing obstructing their view.

After singing through their chorus, a moment of silence followed as everyone seem to be enjoying the view.

The deeper gritty voice of Kindly began to fill the silence with a song of his own, a tune that would have been best accompanied by a banjo:

I like the ground and I love the dirt
When I'm on it, I don't get hurt
It smells like dirt and it makes me dirty
I can stand on it because of gravity

Everyone stared at Kindly for a moment and then the basket erupted with laughter that could be heard by people in the other balloons suspended between the ground and clouds. Patience gave out a little snort when she laughed, and that caused everyone to laugh even harder.

CHAPTER 8

DUSTY ROADS

*And let us take thought of how to spur one another
on to love and good works…*
Hebrews 10:24

Normally crossing the back roads through the fields and forests of the Land of Promise would be a gentle drive with peaceful slopes and winding roads. Today, Pop and Goody's drive was nothing close to slow and peaceful. It resembled bumps and turns of a race car driver attempting to keep the lead during a close pursuit.

Over the sound of Pop's tools and spare parts rattling from all corners of his truck, Goody yelled out so Pop could hear him, "Pop, I see our hot air balloon just over Cattail Bay. If they continue that trajectory, we could have them land in Old Man Kelly's field. He's not planting this year so it is open and available. I believe he is about five miles from the water."

Pop replied in a voice louder than Goody's, "That's a great idea, Goody. Let's see if we can get a little closer so we are in range and get them on the radio to have them begin a slow descent after they fly over the bay."

In Goody's estimation, Pop couldn't speed up anymore but to his surprise, Goody watched the speedometer gain a few ticks.

Pop was narrowing the gap between them and his friends in this hot air balloon chase. As they seemingly inched closer, Goody grew more anxious with the thought of getting his friends to the ground safely. This day did not go as planned but Goody was not about to let his friends feel like they were flying alone. He and Pop were determined to get close enough so they could talk their friends down to the ground.

In that moment, Goody breathed a simple prayer, "God, help us!"

As they continued to drive, every couple minutes Goody would hit the walkie-talkie button and say, "Come in Temperance, come in Jojo, can you hear me? Gen, Charity, Quill, are you there? Come in Kindly. Patience, Faith, can you hear my voice? Can anyone hear me? You guys are going to be alright. We have a plan."

As soon as Pop drove near Cattail Bay, he turned a sharp right and drove around the bay on the shortest route that would lead them to Old Man Kelly's farm. On the long straight stretches, Pop would pick up speed, and when curves in the road would come, he would slow and hug the inner curve. Only one time did they pass some farm equipment, and Pop honked as he drove past to alert the farmer that he was in a rush and to pardon the kicked up dust.

Goody looked behind them and he could see through the trail of dust the other hot air balloons that had taken flight. If he truly had time to look, he would have admired the beautiful sight, but he was blind to the beauty today, keeping his friends in sight. He just wanted to help them safely land. He looked over at his Pop and knew that there was no one better than Pop to get his friends to safety, and he knew that God was going to give them the wisdom they needed to get the group home.

"Come in guys, can you hear me?" Goody tried again.
All at once, he heard some crackle noises, fuzz, and then a voice, "Hello….? Goody? Is … you? C… you….. us?"

CHAPTER 9

LOSING ALTITUDE

Trust in the Lord with all your heart,
and do not rely on your own understanding.
Proverbs 3:5

Quill now had the walkie-talkie in hand and continued to connect with Goody as Temperance poured over his notes. He was studying Temperance's notes and looking up to the mechanisms in the hot air balloon, making sure he understood exactly what needed to be done, when the time was right, he wanted to be ready.

Gen let out a little squeal and everyone jumped. She said with excitement, "I see them! There is Pop and Goody's truck down there next to the water. Look!"

Everyone rushed to the side of the basket and peered over the edge as the basket tipped and rocked in that direction. Sure enough, Pop and Goody was spotted by the group just where Gen was pointing. Circling the bay was Pop's truck leaving a dust trail behind him. It was evident that Pop was driving extremely fast.

Temperance squinted to try and see Pop and Goody more clearly as they were speeding along and remembered about how far apart they were when they lost contact. He decided to close

the distance between them.

Temperance told Kindly, "Reach up to the lever and begin releasing some of the air from the hot air balloon."

Kindly asked Temperance, "Why? Why would we do that?"

Temperance replied, "We have to get closer to Pop and Goody if we are going to be able to communicate with them. The only way I know is to get lower."

"But what if we need that air that you are letting out?" Kindly surmised.

Temperance had a determined look on his face when he said, "I have been looking over everything we talked about and I believe we will be fine if we drop the basket a few hundred feet. We need to steer clear of tall trees but we have plenty of space out here, and it would be good to hear more instructions from Pop.

As the balloon began to drop, they all clapped and cheered when they heard Goody's broken voice over the walkie-talkie. "Come in Temp…., can you ….? Gen, Charity, Quill, …. you there? Come in …You guys are ….. alright. We have a plan."

CHAPTER 10

A FRIEND CALLED MISCHIEVOUS

The one who covers his transgressions will not prosper, but whoever confesses them and forsakes them will find mercy.
Proverbs 28:13

As Feargus walked home, he didn't know the outcome of what was happening to the kids in the hot air balloon. He realized that his actions could have caused some real problems for them. He suddenly felt something he hadn't felt in an extremely long time; he felt remorse. He was sorry for what he had done.

This emotion was something new to him. Normally, he enjoyed making trouble and seeing its effect. He thought it was funny to see people pranked. Not this time. The weight of what he did fell heavy on his shoulders. He didn't like what he was feeling so he decided to brush off this emotion and choose to find the humor in his prank. He muttered to himself, "It was funny. It was funny to see them jostle around in the basket. I really got them! No one will ever know it was me."

When Feargus walked through his front door, his mom called out to him, "Hey Feargus, how was the balloon launch? Did you get to see the hot air balloons all take off?"

Feargus replied, "I watched one balloon launch and it was kind of dumb, so I left."

Surprised by his response his mom said, "Really? I thought you would enjoy it."

Feargus thought for a moment, "Maybe it's cool if you are the one who is actually going up in the balloon, but for the people watching, it's really boring."

His mom shrugged and walked into the kitchen to start making lunch.

Feargus turned towards the stairs and at that moment realized that he was jealous of those kids. They had each other to lean on when the balloon launched too early. They were doing something together. Together. He didn't have a friend who he could have fun adventures with or even lean on when trouble hit. He was alone. But he liked being alone. Didn't he? At least that's what he told himself.

Feargus was surprised by the one single tear that was running down his face. He sniffled, and wiped his cheek leaving a smudge of sand from the sandbag, then turned to go to his room. Tomorrow was a new day and although he didn't have adventures with friends planned, mischievousness was the friend he knew all too well. Feargus began dreaming up his next scheme as he plopped on his bed.

He rolled onto his back and stared at the ceiling. He wondered if the hot air balloon still hung suspended in the sky.

CHAPTER 11

DOWN TO THE TREETOPS

God is our strong refuge; he is truly our helper in times of trouble.
Psalm 46:1

"You are going to land in the field of Old Man Kelly. Over," Goody yelled into the walkie-talkie, hoping they could understand the instructions. "Begin turning down the burner flame so you can cool the air inside the balloon."

Quill repeated the instructions back to Goody over the walkie-talkie. "Turn down flame, got it, over!"

Goody continued, "You should be heading north with the direction of the wind, and after you pass the wooded area beyond the Cattail Bay, turn down the flame even more. Make sure to avoid the tops of the trees. After you pass the trees, you should be able to bring her down in the field, over."

"Okay, miss the trees, land in the field, over." Quill again repeated letting Goody know that he heard and understood the plans. "We will begin a slow descent."

Hearing and understanding is one thing. Doing it all correctly is a whole other issue. Temperance looked at each one of his friends. "Okay guys, we will need to work together to bring the

64

balloon down. Kindly, you will need to man the burner flame."

Kindly, who had started enjoying the balloon ride, quickly snapped into place under the burner, "You got it! I am ready to go here. We've got this!"

Faith smiled. She was so proud of her friend who quickly showed bravery in the face of fear. "Way to go, Kindly!" She remarked. "Temperance, what do you think the rest of us should do?"

Temperance replied, "Quill, you and Gen grab the ladder and throw it over the side once we are past the trees, so that we are ready to climb out when we land."

Quill said, "You got it!"

Gen nodded and gave a thumbs up.

Temperance continued divvying up the responsibilities. He pointed at Joy and said, "JoJo, let's have you make sure all the stakes around the basket are ready to drop in case we need to stake the basket down after we land.

"Patience, I would like for you to watch for any obstacles as we get closer to the ground. You will be our lookout. Let's try and descend at a nice slow rate while avoiding the trees. Stay at the front of where we are heading and keep us posted."

"Faith and Charity, I have a special job for you. You guys should sing our new flying song. I think that will help us stay focused and encouraged. We wrote a song together, we can bring this

hot air balloon down together as well."

Charity giggled and she and Faith began to sing the song softly. "When you fly in the sky…" As they sang, everyone calmed down from any anxiety they were feeling.

Patience said to Temperance, "There is the bay, and I can see the field!"

Temperance gave the instructions to Kindly, "Turn down the flame some more. We have to get closer to the ground. We are still too high."

Kindly lowered the heat and the balloon quickly dropped lower.

Patience spoke with certainty, "Temperance, I think we are getting too low too quick. The trees are close and if we continue going down at this pace, we are going to hit them."

Charity and Faith began to quiet the singing as the tension rose.

In an attempt to correct this problem, Kindly turned up the heat, slowly raising the temperature and the balloon.

Temperance, feeling the strain of not being confident one way or another spoke out in haste. "Kindly, we need to drop lower. Lower the flames."

Kindly, while listening to the instructions he was receiving from his friends and without looking around, focused his full attention on his task at hand, controlling the balloon by lowering the flame again. As he did, Patience inhaled quickly. What sounded like scratches began to vibrate the underside of the basket. They were hitting the tops of the trees. The basket was jostled and everyone began to scream.

ADVENTURERS DESCEND

*Give thanks to the Lord, for he is good,
and his loyal love endures!*
Psalm 107:1

Goody could see that they were too close to the trees. He quickly pushed the button on the walkie-talkie, yelling again into the mouthpiece, "More heat! More heat! You have to get over those trees."

He saw the basket tipping a bit as it scraped the tops of the tallest pine trees. He could hear the distant screams of his friends. Knowing that adjusting the balloons altitude was not instantaneous, he was hoping his instructions would help altar their descent and keep them from getting deeper into the trees.

His heart raced as he watched his friends suspended in the balloon, a ride that was supposed to be fun had turned into a misadventure, for sure! Watching them while being on the ground left him feeling helpless He breathed a prayer again for safety. He knew he may not be able to help at this point, but God could give them wisdom.

A moment later, the balloon had risen enough to clear the tops of the remaining trees. Relieved for a moment, Goody then focused on the next big hurdle - getting them to the ground, without scuff or bruise, safe and sound.

He radioed over the walkie-talkie to his friends, "Great job controlling your descent. You topped a few trees but were able to pull it up in time. I'm proud of you all!"

Pop and Goody heard the walkie chirp and then static. Goody's heart leapt in his chest. Were they all alright? All at once, the static was gone and he could clearly hear Quill over the walkie-talkie, "Goody? Pop? We had a close call there but we managed to pull up before causing damage to the balloon and to us. We are all ready to be on the ground. Can you talk us down?"

Relieved, Goody replied, "You bet! I can't wait to hug each of your necks."

With each passing moment, the balloon descended towards the field where Pop and Goody had predicted.

Goody assured them, "You guys are almost down. Hang on and be prepared, the balloon basket may bounce a little when you land."

Goody continued to talk them through how to prepare for the final moments of touchdown. As the balloon slowly lost heat, it descended, settling down right at the edge of the field, just before the creek.

After dragging across the grass a bit, they finally stopped moving and everyone breathed a sigh of relief. Quill and Gen threw the ladder over the side just as Temperance had instructed, and Quill began helping everyone out of the basket. Pop made

sure each one stepped down from the ladder safely, and Goody greeted each friend with a tight squeeze.

After they all stood on the ground, the group of friends erupted in smiles and laughter. They had done it. They landed safely and were so glad to be together again. A day meant for fun had taken a wrong turn, and through it all, they had worked to make it back to the ground safely.

The midday sun was beginning to warm the air as Pop explained how they would deflate and roll up the balloon. Even being a bit shaken, group listened and worked to put everything away.

As the nylon fabric completely deflated, the hot air balloon lost its shape and power to fly. The balloon sagged and started to fold over to the ground. Moments later, they rolled the nylon fabric up together, and as they did, they retold the events of the morning from their different vantage points. With each perspecitve, the tensions began to melt.

Patience smiled as she remarked, "Goody, you should have seen Kindly. He made us all proud. You know how much he loves being in dirt and yet he was the only one who could reach the burner. He stood up for us and faced his fear. He went from afraid to brave! We are all so proud of him!"

The group nodded in agreement.

Kindly laughed and said, "The thought of being on the ground was a great motivator too! I am glad I was able to help, and I am thankful I had my friends encouraging me to reach up to where I didn't think I could. I was even able to enjoy the view for part of it. It's great to have friends who believe in you!"

Joy giggled and said, "And Temperance led us well with his detailed note-taking and knowledge. We couldn't have made it without him."

"It was only logical that we had all the information down on paper. Thank you, Pop, for explaining everything so well. You gave us all the tools we needed to fly a hot air balloon!"

"Kindly and Temperance are the true heroes today! They worked as a team to get us back on the ground." Quill stated.

Pop, who had been listening intently to the kids retell their adventure, proudly announced, "Sounds like you all worked as a team to be the heroes of your story. Great job today! Let's take a minute and be grateful for God's guidance and safety today as well."

Goody walked over to his Pop and gave him a big hug and began to pray, "Thank you, God, for bringing my friends safely down to the ground. Thank you for Pop giving such great instructions, and to us for being good listeners. Help us to always be grateful. Amen."

All the kids said, "Amen," and then laughed together. They were so grateful they had their friends to lean on when the day became difficult and that this unexpected adventure had come to end.

EPILOGUE

SING IT AGAIN

Give thanks to the Lord! Call on his name!
Make known his accomplishments among the nations!
Psalm 105:1

The next day, Pop invited the group of friends to the park for a barbecue to give everyone time to share about the day before. He wanted to hear all about their experience. This was the first time his hot air balloon went up without him, so he couldn't wait for details of how they worked as a team.

As they sat down at the picnic table for some lunch, Goody expressed again how proud he was of everyone. "You guys really did a great job remembering all the tools you were taught and not forgetting your wits yesterday."

Charity spoke up first, "I was so glad that Kindly had the courage to stand up to his fear. He put aside himself to think of his friends who needed him."

"And Temperance," Faith continued, "showed us how important it is to pay attention and use what we learn to get out of trouble."

"Yes, because of his notes, we all became song writers," Quill chuckled.

Goody looked puzzled, "What? Songwriters? What are you talking about?"

Joy laughed, "Temperance reminded us that we were supposed to make a memory. That's what Pop said to do. We were all a little afraid so I explained that when I am afraid, I write a song. Together we wrote a song about our time in the clouds. It calmed us all down and gave us a reason to laugh."

"I must hear that song!" Goody laughed.

Pop agreed, "Yes, we have to hear this song. Often times when faced with adversity, good things are birthed."

Joy began singing, just as she had started the day before. The others joined into the song, even Kindly, who wasn't part of the original song, sang out with gusto.

When we fly in the sky
Where the clouds and the birds go by
The wind controls the places we go
Adventure awaits so enjoy the show

When we fly in the sky
We can't believe what we see with our eyes
Our homes below, so tiny and small
Mountains are hills, nothing is tall

At the end of the song, Kindly sang the song he had made up in the midst of his fear.

I like the ground and I love the dirt

When I'm on it, I don't get hurt
It smells like dirt and it makes me dirty
I can stand on it because of gravity

Everyone erupted in laughter at Kindly's deep voice singing his made up jingle. It may have been inspired by the flight of the wayward balloon, but no truer words could be spoken about Kindly's love of dirt.

As they cleaned up their lunch from the picnic table, Goody remarked, "Pop, what I can't figure out is how that balloon let loose. I know we had everything secured properly. What do you think happened?"

Pop, with an inquisitive look on his face responded, "It's a mystery for sure. We may never know. But for today, let's be grateful for our friends and their safety."

Until our next adventure…

THE END!

A Land of Promise Adventure | Book 2

The MISADVENTURE of the BLUSTERY WIND

PARENT & TEACHER HELPS

TABLE OF CONTENTS
PARENT & TEACHER HELPS

Prologue | Fear Finds a Voice 82

Chapter 1 | Safety First 84

Chapter 2 | Friend…Foe…or Fear 86

Chapter 3 | Anticipation 88

Chapter 4 | Mischievousness Gone Wrong 90

Chapter 5 | Heat Always Rises 92

Chapter 6 | Mapping a Landing 94

Chapter 7 | Make a Memory 96

Chapter 8 | Dusty Roads 98

Chapter 9 | Losing Altitude 100

Chapter 10 | A Friend Called Mischievous 102

Chapter 11 | Down to the Treetops 104

Chapter 12 | Adventurers Descend 106

Epilogue | Sing it Again 108

HOW TO USE THIS GUIDE

This "Helps Section" is designed to give a simple yet practical tool to connect the story with real-life conversations through applications, questions, and activities. Each chapter's helps are designed to spark discussion, invite reflection, and give avenues to practice the Fruit of the Spirit at school, at home, and with friends. Use these with your child, in a classroom, or in a small group to deepen learning and inspire growth!

Here's what you will find:

- Big Idea: The main lesson or theme from the story.

- Fruit of the Spirit Highlighted: Which Fruit of the Spirit is seen in action.

- Talk About It: Discussion questions to spark conversation.

- Live It Out: Practical ways kids can apply the lesson in daily life.

- Creative Connection: Crafts or activities to reinforce the story.

- Read these Bible Verses: Bible verses that tie directly to the theme.

PROLOGUE

FEAR FINDS A VOICE

BIG IDEA

Feeling left out can twist into fear and meanness—but God can redirect our hearts toward belonging and kindness.

FRUIT OF THE SPIRIT HIGHLIGHTED

Self-Control: What does it look like when we don't use self-control? Feargus lets fear and hurt drive his choices. Instead of managing his emotions, he chooses to hurt others with pranks and showing meanness.

TALK ABOUT IT

1. Why does Feargus start doing pranks?
2. When have you felt left out? What helped?
3. What's the difference between being "tough" and being truly brave?
4. If Feargus had one safe friend, how might things have changed?

LIVE IT OUT

- **At School:** Notice a lonely classmate; invite them into a game or conversation.

- **At Home:** Trade "attention-getting" with "encouragement-giving": Give two separate people compliments today.

- **With Friends:** If you are put in a situation where you need to pause and think of the best way forward, practice a three second pause before reacting. (Pause, breathe, say a prayer, and move forward with a positive outlook.)

CREATIVE CONNECTION

Turn the Lie Around: On one side of a card write a fear or negative thought (e.g., "No one likes me" or "I'm not good at something"), on the back write a truth (e.g., "God loves me" or "I can continue to become better at something").

Belonging Web: In a group setting, sit in a circle, hold a ball of yarn and keep one end of the yarn. Say something about yourself and find someone that has something in common with you (e.g., I like to eat pizza.) Throw the ball of yarn to the person that shares what you state. Continue around the room until everyone has had a chance. Look around the room and see how you are all connected.

READ THESE BIBLE VERSES:

1 Corinthians 13:4 – Love is patient, love is kind…
Galatians 5:22–23 – But the fruit of the Spirit is love, joy, peace, patience, kindness, goodness, faithfulness, gentleness, and self-control.
Romans 12:21 – Do not be overcome by evil, but overcome evil with good.

CHAPTER 1

SAFETY FIRST

BIG IDEA

Preparation along with prayer help to build and bring peace before trying a new adventure.

FRUIT OF THE SPIRIT HIGHLIGHTED

Peace: Pop models how God's peace can settle fear before a big adventure. Pop brings a calmness to the nervous group. He prays, explains safety, and reassures them about the balloon ride.

TALK ABOUT IT

1. How did Pop model safety and trust in God?
2. Why does training matter?
3. How does praying together change the atmosphere in a group setting?
4. Which safety fact stuck with you most?
5. Where do you need better preparation this week?

LIVE IT OUT

- **At School:** Is your class going on a field trip? Make a mini "safety plan" for the trip that models being safe.

- **On Your Team:** Start a game, match, or meet with a short prayer.

- **At Home:** Choose one role you'll own and finish it. (e.g., dishwasher, bathroom cleaner).

CREATIVE CONNECTION

Balloon Basics Diagram: Draw a hot air balloon, decorate it with a special design, and label the different parts of the balloon with the different parts of the balloon that Pop told the kids about (e.g., envelope, burner, basket). Which part of the balloon is your favorite to draw?

Prayer Jar: Decorate a jar, box, or container. Write prayer requests on popsicle sticks. As you are praying, pull out the popsicle sticks, one at a time, and spend time praying over each prayer in your jar.

READ THESE BIBLE VERSES:

James 1:5 – But if anyone is deficient in wisdom, he should ask God, who gives to all generously and without reprimand, and it will be given to him.

Philippians 4:6–7 – Do not be anxious about anything. Instead, in every situation, through prayer and petition with thanksgiving, tell your requests to God.

Proverbs 21:5 – The plans of the diligent lead only to plenty, but everyone who is hasty comes only to poverty.

CHAPTER 2

FRIEND...FOE...OR FEAR

BIG IDEA

Hurt people can sometimes hurt people; God's love can heal the hurting.

FRUIT OF THE SPIRIT HIGHLIGHTED

Love: We can see how lack of love can twist a heart—and why loving others matters. What happens when Feargus doesn't receive love and kindness? Being mocked at the park shapes his view of people and himself.

TALK ABOUT IT

1. What early moment shaped Feargus?
2. How did rejection turn into jealousy?
3. How can we be kind and set boundaries?
4. Where could Feargus have asked for help?
5. What's a kinder choice Feargus could make next time?

LIVE IT OUT

- **At School:** When encountering a situation where someone crosses a boundary, practice communicating that boundary: (e.g., "That wasn't kind. Please stop.")

- **At Home:** Write a short prayer for someone who's hard to love.

- **With Friends:** List three people you can ask for help when you feel left out.

CREATIVE CONNECTION

Upside-down Heart: Draw a heart on a piece of paper. Turn the heart upside down and write Feargus's negative words or emotions that show he is sad and/or wounded, then turn the heart over and draw a line and write out on top of those words what God says about each of us with "healing words." What God says about you is more powerful than the feelings.
Baked Clay Craft: Mold clay into a heart or hot air balloon and write a word on the image that is something you want in a friend. Bake it in the oven on a cookie sheet, with the help of an adult. Paint the baked clay to decorate.

READ THESE BIBLE VERSES:

Ephesians 4:31–32 – You must put away every kind of bitterness, anger, wrath, quarreling, and evil, slanderous talk. Instead, be kind to one another, compassionate, forgiving one another, just as God in Christ also forgave you.
Luke 6:27–28 – But I say to you who are listening: Love your enemies, do good to those who hate you, bless those who curse you, pray for those who mistreat you.
Romans 12:18 – If possible, so far as it depends on you, live peaceably with all people.

CHAPTER 3

ANTICIPATION

BIG IDEA

Patience and encouragement help us to wait well.

FRUIT OF THE SPIRIT HIGHLIGHTED

Patience: An example of "waiting well" vs. anxious and fidgety waiting. The kids have to wait for Pop and Goody to return and for the launch time. They're excited, nervous, and waiting while in the hot air balloon basket.

TALK ABOUT IT

1. Of the friends, who did you find was the most encouraging, while they waited?
2. How did Temperance's planning help?
3. Why did Kindly struggle—and how did his friends respond?
4. What helps you wait calmly?
5. What have you done that made you excited and nervous at the same time?

LIVE IT OUT

- **At School:** Encourage someone who's anxious with one sentence of hope.

- **At Home:** When you come in from being outside of your home, create a calm-down routine that gets you ready for the next task (e.g., Put away your coat and shoes, take a deep breath, grab a glass of water).

- **At a Store:** You may find yourself in a long line at the grocery or department store, use positive words while waiting. No complaining allowed.

CREATIVE CONNECTION

Waiting Toolkit: You will find yourself waiting many times in a week. What are some ways to fill your time? Create a list of things you can do to fill your time that are encouraging, patient, or represents you are waiting well. Write these items down on index cards. If you find yourself waiting, draw a card and do the item you wrote on the card.

Thankful and Grateful: Who is one person you are thankful for this week. Write a thank you card to that person and put it in the mail.

READ THESE BIBLE VERSES:

Psalm 27:14 – Rely on the Lord ! Be strong and confident! Rely on the Lord!

Romans 15:5 – Now may the God of endurance and comfort give you unity with one another in accordance with Christ Jesus…

Colossians 3:15 – Let the peace of Christ be in control in your heart (for you were in fact called as one body to this peace), and be thankful.

CHAPTER 4

MISCHIEVOUSNESS GONE WRONG

BIG IDEA

Small wrongs can cause big consequences; integrity protects everyone.

FRUIT OF THE SPIRIT HIGHLIGHTED

Goodness: Choices affect others—why goodness matters. Feargus secretly damages the sandbags. His choice nearly causes disaster. In contrast, Pop and Goody rush to find a resolution and be a help in time of need.

TALK ABOUT IT

1. What chain reaction followed after Feargus's poor choice when he sabotaged the sandbags?
2. What could Feargus have done instead with his feelings?
3. How did Pop and Goody respond—panic or purpose?
4. When have you realized a choice made had greater consequences than you first realized?
5. One poor decision or one good decision can affect those around you. Name one good decision that affects others in a positive way.

LIVE IT OUT

- **At School:** Commit to one integrity choice today by choosing to tell the truth, return something you borrowed, help repair something broken.

- **At Home:** We can act out in many ways but if you sense you are becoming jealous of someone, make a plan to not allow those feelings to overtake or overwhelm you.

- **With Friends:** Apologize quickly when you mess up. Don't allow ill feelings to linger.

CREATIVE CONNECTION

Domino Choices: With a domino set, build a chain of dominoes around your space close enough to knock one down with the next domino. Once the dominoes are lined up in a row, topple one domino to see how long it takes for all the dominoes to fall. Compare how long it took to set up?

Pick Up Sticks Game: Using popsicle sticks, wooden skewers, chopsticks, or Pick Up Sticks, drop the sticks in a pile. Try and pull a stick without moving any other stick, other than the one you are touching. How hard is it to only affect the movement of one stick?

READ THESE BIBLE VERSES:

Proverbs 10:9 – The one who conducts himself in integrity will live securely, but the one who behaves perversely will be found out.

Philippians 2:3–4 – Instead of being motivated by selfish ambition or vanity, each of you should, in humility, be moved to treat one another as more important than yourself.

CHAPTER 5

HEAT ALWAYS RISES

BIG IDEA

Courage is doing what's needed, even scared.

FRUIT OF THE SPIRIT HIGHLIGHTED

Faith: Remember to have faith in God and others. Acting on what we've been taught, even when scared. In the chaos, Temperance goes back to Pop's notes, Kindly obeys even though he's scared, and they trust Goody's voice.

TALK ABOUT IT

1. What helped Kindly stand up to fear?
2. How did the team use their training under stress?
3. Why did clear roles matter?
4. What words boosted courage?
5. What helps you to be brave even when you're scared?

LIVE IT OUT

- **At School:** Next time you have a class assignment that includes a group, be one of the first to take ownership and name your role out loud.

- **At Home:** Sometimes we can be clearer in our communication. What's one area you can be clearer in your communication? Start with using this walkie-talkie phrase at home: "Checking in!"

- **With Friends:** Give yourself an opportunity to walk in a courageous way. Go out of your way to help someone do something that you would be fearful of doing alone (e.g., hike a mountain, try a new sport, eat something different than your are use to.)

CREATIVE CONNECTION

Courage Mirror: What is one task that you are struggling to complete or an area you need courage? Write it down on a sticky note and add it to your bathroom mirror. Read the task out loud everyday until you complete it.

New Recipe Challenge: Trying something new can be scary but you are challenged to try a new recipe with an adult and see if this is a thumbs up or thumbs down food you would try again or never eat again.

READ THESE BIBLE VERSES:

Joshua 1:9 – I repeat, be strong and brave! Don't be afraid and don't panic, for I, the Lord your God, am with you in all you do."

2 Timothy 1:7 – For God did not give us a Spirit of fear but of power and love and self-control.

Psalm 56:3 – When I am afraid, I trust in you.

CHAPTER 6

MAPPING A LANDING

BIG IDEA

Wise mentors along with clear guidance will help you stay steady on a journey of uncertainty.

FRUIT OF THE SPIRIT HIGHLIGHTED

Goodness: Goodness is not just "being nice"—it's actively doing what is right for others. Pop and Goody don't waste time blaming each other or the situation. They plan, chase the balloon, and do everything they can to protect the kids.

TALK ABOUT IT

1. What did Pop/Goody do well while under pressure?
2. Who mentors you?
3. What value do you find listening?
4. When have you found you need outside guidance?

LIVE IT OUT

- **At School:** Ask a trusted adult a "teach-me" question this week and be ready to listen and learn.

- **At Home:** Practice repeating back instructions.

- **With Friends:** Thank a friend with a note of gratitude.

CREATIVE CONNECTION

Weather the Storm: Watch the weather report. Are there storms that show up in the forecast? How would you prepare for a storm near you?

Days & Months: What's your favorite month of the year? How many days in that month? Draw out a calendar for that month and put in any special events that are planned for that month. Have you planned ahead for those events? How can you start planning now for those days?

READ THESE BIBLE VERSES:

Proverbs 19:20 – Listen to advice and receive discipline, that you may become wise by the end of your life.

Psalm 32:8 – I will instruct and teach you about how you should live. I will advise you as I look you in the eye.

Hebrews 13:7 – Remember your leaders, who spoke God's message to you; reflect on the outcome of their lives and imitate their faith.

CHAPTER 7

MAKE A MEMORY

BIG IDEA

Knowing your purpose behind an adventure can lead you to new heights and you may even be challenged to find new talents.

FRUIT OF THE SPIRIT HIGHLIGHTED

Joy: Joy isn't pretending everything is fine; it's choosing to celebrate God's goodness in the middle of hard things. In the middle of fear, the kids choose to "make a memory" and write a silly song. They laugh together even when faced with hard things.

TALK ABOUT IT

1. Why did singing help the friends in the hot air balloon?
2. What beauty did they notice?
3. What's a memory you want to "keep"?
4. How can gratitude change a hard moment?

LIVE IT OUT

- **At School:** There may be hard days at school, but even on those days, find three reasons to be grateful.

- **At Home:** When you are feeling anxious, ask an adult how they handle moments that they are stressed.

- **With Friends:** What amazed you about today? Share your "wonder moment" with a friend.

CREATIVE CONNECTION

Write a Song: Using your creative writing skills, write a 4-line song and give it a tune. Sing it to your friends or family. It may be funny or silly, but putting words in a song may help you write down your emotions.

Airy Balloon: Blow up two balloons. You and a friend will have a competition. Each person will tap the balloon into the air and keep it up as long as you can without allowing it to touch the ground. The one who keeps the balloon up the longest wins.

READ THESE BIBLE VERSES:

Psalm 77:11–12 – I will remember the works of the Lord . Yes, I will remember the amazing things you did long ago!

Colossians 3:16 – Let the word of Christ dwell in you richly, teaching and exhorting one another with all wisdom, singing psalms, hymns, and spiritual songs, all with grace in your hearts to God.

CHAPTER 8

DUSTY ROADS

BIG IDEA

Perseverance encourages you to move toward people, not away from your problems.

FRUIT OF THE SPIRIT HIGHLIGHTED

Kindness: Kindness is steady, gentle words that remind others they're not alone. Goody's constant encouraging words over the walkie-talkie: "You guys are going to be alright. We have a plan," helped everyone realize they were going to be alright.

TALK ABOUT IT

1. How did Pop drive with purpose but care?
2. Why did Goody keep calling on the radio?
3. What does "closing the gap" look like in friendships?
4. Who do you need to move toward this week?
5. What does it look like to you for love to keep trying?

LIVE IT OUT

- **At School:** You may know someone who is currently struggling with something. Check in on that person this week.

- **At Home:** Have you made a promise to someone you still

haven't kept? Keep a promise you made.

- **With Friends:** Try again at something you've avoided in a friendship. Do you need to forgive, confront, or have a conversation?

CREATIVE CONNECTION

I'm Packing For My Trip: For your next road trip, play this fun game. The first person says "I'm packing for my trip, and I'm bringing [something that starts with the letter A, like apples]." The next person repeats what the first person said, then adds on something that starts with the letter B. Continue through the alphabet. The game continues with each person having to remember and repeat what's already been said and then adding on something that starts with the next letter of the alphabet.

READ THESE BIBLE VERSES:

Galatians 6:9 – So we must not grow weary in doing good, for in due time we will reap, if we do not give up.
Hebrews 10:24 – And let us take thought of how to spur one another on to love and good works…

CHAPTER 9

LOSING ALTITUDE

BIG IDEA

Sometimes you must slow down, listen, and lower your pride to actually hear when help is being offered.

FRUIT OF THE SPIRIT HIGHLIGHTED

Self-Control: Self-control requires thinking before acting, especially under pressure.

TALK ABOUT IT

1. Finding balance in the midst of difficult situations can be challenging. How would you have stayed calm while bringing the balloon down?
2. What seemed risky concerning lowering the balloon?
3. How do you stay in range with wise voices?
4. When do you need to turn the volume down on fear?
5. Name a time in your life that you had to ask for someone to help you with advice?

LIVE IT OUT

- **At School:** Surround yourself with friends who give great advice.

- **At Home:** When trouble comes up or a decision needs to be made, ask for advice from a trusted person.

- **With Friends:** Pride goes alone, but being humble brings someone along. Replace the phrase, "I got this!" with "Let's do this."

CREATIVE CONNECTION

Fireworks Painting: Using a straw, spread paint, creating effects that look like fireworks or abstract designs by watering down paint to a liquid consistency. Use a spoon or dropper to place a few drops of the watery paint onto a piece of paper. Use a straw to blow a strong burst of air onto the paint blob, spreading it out across the paper. Add more drops of paint and repeat until you achieve the desired firework effect.

READ THESE BIBLE VERSES:

Proverbs 3:5 – Trust in the Lord with all your heart, and do not rely on your own understanding.
James 1:19 – Understand this, my dear brothers and sisters! Let every person be quick to listen, slow to speak, slow to anger.

CHAPTER 10

A FRIEND CALLED MISCHIEVOUS

BIG IDEA

Conviction is a gift; it alerts us when we need to make a change, gives opportunity to confess poor choices, and leads us to better choices.

FRUIT OF THE SPIRIT HIGHLIGHTED

Goodness: Feargus feels genuine remorse. He realizes he could have caused serious harm, and it bothers him deeply. He was almost repentant. This is the first step toward change—when God nudges our hearts that something we did was wrong

TALK ABOUT IT

1. What new feeling surprised Feargus?
2. How is remorse different from shame?
3. Why is jealousy loud but emptiness louder?
4. What would confession look like for Feargus?
5. Who could help him make it right?

LIVE IT OUT

- **At School:** Think of one area where you need to repair a relationship. Follow that up with action to fix what has been broken.

- **At Home:** Need to say you're sorry? Practice a 3-part apology: "I'm sorry for ____. It was wrong because ____. Next time I will ____."

- **With Friends:** Pray for courage to tell the truth.

CREATIVE CONNECTION

Every Other Art: With a friend, each of you start a drawing on separate pieces of paper. Every three minutes, switch your art with each other. Continue switching until the picture is complete. What challenges came up while were drawing?
Telling the Truth? With a friend, each of you secretly grab an object. Don't show the object to the other person. Each one will describe the object in every detail without saying what it is, but you have a choice to make, are you going to add in a little untruth about the description? At the end of each of your descriptions, the wiinner guesses item and whether or not the describer was telling the whole truth about the object

READ THESE BIBLE VERSES:

1 John 1:9 – But if we confess our sins, he is faithful and righteous, forgiving us our sins and cleansing us from all unrighteousness.
Proverbs 28:13 – The one who covers his transgressions will not prosper, but whoever confesses them and forsakes them will find mercy.

CHAPTER 11

DOWN TO THE TREETOPS

BIG IDEA

In moments of tension, lean into your friends for strength by your willingness to listen to their advice and open to pivot when those you trust speak out to help.

FRUIT OF THE SPIRIT HIGHLIGHTED

Kindness: Kindness is often practical: sharing the load, using your gifts for the team. All the friends support each other by doing a job that helps the group. Through their encouragement, they sing to calm fears, and work together to land.

TALK ABOUT IT

1. What almost went wrong—and what saved the day?
2. How did knowing who was doing what role matter?
3. What's the danger of mixed messages under stress?
4. Which kid did you most identify with when they were over the treetops?
5. What did you learn about listening while leading?

LIVE IT OUT

- **At School:** Sometimes directions can be confusing. When you have been given directions you are still trying to understand, practice repeating the directions before acting.

- **At Home:** Plan ahead for moments of disagreements. Pick a "calm word" to pause and reset if you find you are in the middle of a disagreement at home.

- **With Friends:** Do you have someone who looks out for you? They are always helping to remind you, warn you, or encourage you. Thank the "lookouts" in your life with a kind word.

CREATIVE CONNECTION

Listen Closely Obstacle Course: Create an obstacle course outside or in a large room. Place obstacles in the area and blindfold someone. Using calm words, guide the person through the obstacle course with calm and precise words. To make it more challenging, have several teams playing at the same time. Listen closely for the person who's voice is guiding you.

READ THESE BIBLE VERSES:

Isaiah 30:21 – You will hear a word spoken behind you, saying, "This is the correct way, walk in it," whether you are heading to the right or the left.

Proverbs 15:1 – A gentle response turns away anger, but a harsh word stirs up wrath.

Psalm 46:1–2 – God is our strong refuge; he is truly our helper in times of trouble. For this reason we do not fear when the earth shakes, and the mountains tumble into the depths of the sea…

CHAPTER 12

ADVENTURERS DESCEND

BIG IDEA

From the intense conclusion to their blustery journey, the kids understand true gratitude as they find peace.

FRUIT OF THE SPIRIT HIGHLIGHTED

Peace: A beautiful moment of peace and grateful reflection as the kids land safe and sound following their crazy adventure. They are grateful to God for His guidance and Pop's teaching.

TALK ABOUT IT

1. What are you most grateful for today?
2. Who did you feel grew the most from this experience?
3. Why is debriefing important?
4. What do you hope to remember the next time you are in a crisis?
5. Remember Pop's prayer? How did God answer it?

LIVE IT OUT

- **At School:** End hard days with a gratitude circle.

- **At Home:** Save one "memory" (ticket/leaf/pic) to remember God's help.

- **With Friends:** Write a thank-you card to someone who you have learned from.

CREATIVE CONNECTION

Balloon Bookmark: Draw a tall and skinny hot air balloon, the size of a bookmark. Write your favorite Bible verse on it, one that helps you remember to stay calm in tough situations. Color the bookmark and keep it in your Bible or chapter book as a reminder of God's provision in your life.
Bible Verse Rock Garden: Using a permanent marker, write some of the verses we have read over the past few chapters. Color and decorate the rocks. Place the rocks in a garden area and remember God's Word is a foundation for living and He can be trusted to help in time of need.

READ THESE BIBLE VERSES:

1 Thessalonians 5:16 – And we have come to know and to believe the love that God has in us. God is love, and the one who resides in love resides in God, and God resides in him. Psalm 107:1 – Give thanks to the Lord, for he is good, and his loyal love endures!

EPILOGUE

SING IT AGAIN

BIG IDEA

Remember together, rejoice together, and keep making room for others.

FRUIT OF THE SPIRIT HIGHLIGHTED

Joy: The shared stories brought laughter. The friends celebrate together with a BBQ, telling the story of how they worked together during adversity, through singing their song and affirming each other's courage and growth.

TALK ABOUT IT

1. Pop said that "good things are birthed from adversity." What do you think that means?
2. The kids said they were "grateful." What does it mean to be grateful?
3. What tradition could keep your friendships strong?
4. The group talked about teamwork. What does "working together" look like to you?
5. Why do you think they invited Pop and Goody to hear their story and song?
6. How does sharing stories bring people closer?

LIVE IT OUT

- **At School:** Have you noticed someone new or someone you don't know? Invite one new person to your next fun plan.

- **At Home:** Come up with one tradition that you can do together to bring your family closer (e.g., eating dinner around a table together, board game night, going for a walk).

- **With Friends:** Share your story: tell someone how God helped you this week.

CREATIVE CONNECTION

Friendship Placemats: Create placemats for a get together. Use construction paper, markers, stickers, and clear contact paper. Write the title at the top, "I am grateful for my friends" and write or draw what you are grateful for on the placemat. Cover with clear contact paper to make it durable.

READ THESE BIBLE VERSES:

Romans 12:16 – Live in harmony with one another; do not be haughty but associate with the lowly. Do not be conceited.
Psalm 105:1 – Give thanks to the Lord! Call on his name! Make known his accomplishments among the nations!

About the Author

Shellie Wooten and her husband live in Salt Lake City, Utah. She is an author of several children's books—with more on the way—and loves using creativity to plant seeds of truth in the next generation. She is the proud mom of four children and delighted with her grandchildren who lovingly call her "Honey." She treasures her role as a pastor's wife and considers it a true joy to serve both the church and an amazing God. If you want to learn more about the Land of Promise friends or books, visit: www.landofpromisebooks.com

Want more titles by this author?
Check out other books by Shellie Wooten:

In the Land of Promise, parade day is finally here! Two groups of kids arrive with big ideas and even bigger hopes—but when one float breaks down and another doesn't quite qualify, it looks like both dreams may come to an end. With creativity, the best solutions often come when people work together.

A blustery wind, a bad choice, and a balloon that launches early send eight friends on an unexpected sky-high adventure. With courage, teamwork, and faith, they learn how to face fear and discover that even unexpected adventures can become powerful ways to overcome fear.

A heartwarming story about a snail's special day and the emotions he felt. As Simon the Snail experiences challenges leading up to his birthday celebration, he learns a valuable lesson on how to manage his emotions and not allow circumstances to change his positive outlook on life.